WRITTEN ECSTASIES

A COLLECTION OF SHORT STORIES

NEELDIP BAROT

Copyright © Neeldip Barot
All Rights Reserved.

This book has been published with all efforts taken to make the material error-free after the consent of the author. However, the author and the publisher do not assume and hereby disclaim any liability to any party for any loss, damage, or disruption caused by errors or omissions, whether such errors or omissions result from negligence, accident, or any other cause.

While every effort has been made to avoid any mistake or omission, this publication is being sold on the condition and understanding that neither the author nor the publishers or printers would be liable in any manner to any person by reason of any mistake or omission in this publication or for any action taken or omitted to be taken or advice rendered or accepted on the basis of this work. For any defect in printing or binding the publishers will be liable only to replace the defective copy by another copy of this work then available.

Writing this collection has been a journey within myself, I thank all the people who have showered love on me that allowed this book to be completed, my parents Amar Barot, Chetna Barot, my brothers Abhijit barot, Parthdeep dhillon have played a vital role and along with me was a beautiful Aura that propelled me to converge my thoughts.

Walking alone takes you far outside,

Walking with people you love takes you further within.

-Neeldip

Contents

CHAPTER ONE

The Soul Sculptor

Lights had surpassed the silhouette of human suffering, or at least it seemed so from the brim, sitting at the coastline of New York harbor looking far beyond till the eyes could seamlessly perceive into the dark, Noah said.

“There must be a way out!!”

“Maybe there is, you just don’t want to see” William said looking at the glittering reflections on volatile water.

“Yeah.... That person you mentioned, that’s just a lie”

“What bad could possibly happen, you don’t have much to lose after what happened” William said looking at Noah with a sterile glance.

“I don’t know, have a bad feeling about this”

“Then you must try, cause you are in this because of one”

“Where can I find this man?”

“There is a ridge outside the city across the river bank, it’s densely foiled they say that’s where he dwells”

That night Noah moved in space to reach the place William mentioned, probably night wasn't the best time to have endeavors there, Noah thought, but it was too late now. He shrugged his feet forward clearing through the tall grass beneath the towering trees, as he reached at an elevated rock, he saw a cave above and went inside.

The night wasn't doing any favors in distorting the vision, further hurled by the ominous cave, a constant ticking sound came from within the cave as he moved forward searching for a presence and shouted.

"Is there any sculptor here!!!!" No one replied except his own voice hurling back.

Again he shouted "sculptor!!" but the result was the same, after a while he heard the sound of water inside the cave and followed it, at the conclusion he found a small torrent pondering into a round pond, he took a glance at it and called again.

"I have come in search of the sculptor, the soul sculptor!!"

As his shout came to an end a voice dense enough to fill the space yet calm as the water flowing around, came from behind.

"You have come to the right place, seeker, I am whom you call.... the soul sculptor"

Deducing the mysterious voice Noah turned to find the origin of it, he took a few steps back looking at the figure as he kept approaching, emerged from the dark a man wearing a robe, his dark hair stretched along his neck and had the face sharp as edge, the sculptor sat on a rock, watching Noah's eyes and asked.

"You look tensed seeker"

Noah trembled with fear at first but the voice made him calm, he asked with hope.

"I have heard that you have the knowledge that answers all questions known to men"

"I do possess the knowledge you seek but it comes at a cost"

Noah took out a deck of bills from his pocket and said

"This is all I have"

"It is not what I asked, the cost is far more greater"

"I don't understand"

"No one does...., what is it that I can be a catalyst in"

Noah came forward and said in a hopeful voice.

"I am in a great debt, a series of many regretful decisions, I have lost the love of my life as a consequence, it is said you can change a person's past, I am a person who needs that change"

"You seek more than a question answered easily, but are you ready to pay the price I ask, seeker" the sculptor stood up and moved toward the pond.

"What is left for anyone to take from me...."

"I am waiting for an answer"

"What is the price?"

"You will know when it's time"

"What if I can't pay"

"You will, there is no other way, drown in this pond and you will wander in your past to change it as your will"

"Just that's it, how much time will I have in my past"

"Until you drown completely, fear not I will pull you out before it is too late"

"I have just you to trust now"

Noah walked to the pond and took a dip by closing his eyes in the chilling water and as he went deeper the water began to feel warm, after a while of sensation he opened his eyes sitting on a bench in the middle of New York, he looked around and there were people going about, he got up and rushed to the newspaper stand across the road, picked up a paper and saw the date of 7 years ago.

He ran to the stock exchange and canceled his investment he did on a stock which would have collapsed down in an hour, He closed his eyes again and opened it at a train station and saw a campaign poster on the ground with date from 5 years ago, he rushed to the real estate broker and canceled the deal of land which he brought and had it's value dropped, he closed his eyes again and opened it in the stock exchange and brought majority of the shares of a firm which was going to escalate, he again closed his eyes and opened it on an alley as he moved around the corner and took a huge amount of money from the drug lord for placing a bet, while he was going to place the bet on the horse which won, he rushed to his bank and checked the balance, which was far more than what he did at that time, he took all the money out, and just as he placed a bet on the horse which was going to win, he felt like he was being starved for breath, he kept trying but found no surface, and as he was going to pass out a hand grabbed him and pulled him out.

Noah found himself within the cave beside the pond with no one around, he called for the sculptor but no one responded, he rushed outside the cave to his home, people on the roads recognized him as they turned their heads to watch him, upon reaching where he lived, he found out that he no longer lives there and found the address of his new home, which turned out to be a luxurious villa, he found his love inside waiting for him, she asked.

"What took you so long, been waiting for you"

Noah didn't answer as the television caught his attention, he saw that he has now became a known businessman and investor, he had articles written about him in popular magazines, at first he couldn't believe what has happened but slowly caught the pace.

Years passed and Noah's life moved ahead, with passing time he became indulged in his business but couldn't maintain his wealth to the same stature and it kept diminishing, after 17 years from the incident he felt that he could make an even bigger fortune and stop his wealth from depleting further, he took to the way of the cave once again and wandered to the foliage, now it was not much green and rich but was still largely untouched by humans, he went inside the cave but this time there was no ticking sound, he started to call the sculptor but no one responded, after a while he heard the torrent voice, he ran following it, he found the pond but the sculptor was not there, he thought he knew what to do, and just as he took the dip in the pond he began to suffocate and his eyes were spread wide open as a hand pulled him out.

Being pulled out from the pond he looked around and saw the sculptor, he looked at himself he was still 25 years old, he tried to analyse what happened and asked the sculptor in amusement.

“What has happened”

“You’ve found the answer, seeker”

“I don’t understand”

“No one does”

“Make me understand then”

“You have changed nothing seeker, not the past nor the future, I just helped you see the problem, the truth, the question was never that you didn’t had enough wealth, the question was you never had enough, the problem was never the debt the problem was you all along, no matter how much you had, you came for more, you family left you again not for what you didn’t had but for what you had, you believed that wealth is the solution cause debt was the problem but you were the problem and knowledge is the solution”

“You mean to say I must change myself”

“If you can, yes”

“What about the price I must pay to you”

“You already did, I have burdened you with the knowledge that you are indeed the problem and the problem is not the mirage you create to hide that, and not everybody has the power to harness the knowledge bestowed upon”

“I will change myself, that is not a problem”

“You can try...., you should be leaving now”

As Noah began to walk away he turned and asked the sculptor.

“You know everything, how you ended in a place like this”

“I just told you, too much knowledge is not easy to harness”.

CHAPTER TWO

NOISES

"It is said that beauty is in the beholder's eyes, but this certainly exists outside (laughs) just look at this mesmerizing view" Sam said standing at the edge of a cliff with warm winds gushing around his long hairs as he looked far into the deserted valley of Arizona with his binoculars.

"I agree with you but we've taken too long of a break; still got an extensive way ahead, should better get back on the road soon" Marie exclaimed resting her hand on the bike.

"Ah.... as you say, always"

"Take this helmet I don't want you to forget me upon falling (Laughs)" Marie tossed the helmet toward Sam.

As they both embarked on the road ahead evening grew over them, midst the vast open night sky, stars glimmered with pondering rays, winds began to reflect a speck of arctic, they kept going for the road ahead was long.

It was 5:30 AM when they arrived at a diversion as two roads diverged before them, Sam asked.

"Which way guide?"

"I am not quite sure... yes, take the right; the left one is not properly mapped and should be a bit longer" Marie said looking at the map.

"Okay so left one it is"

"RIGHTTTT"

"The journey is more important than destination (laughs) and a couple of hours will make no difference, the river will be with us too; there's no debate" Sam said ignoring Marie's voice.

After riding through the changing atmospheres in the valleys of Arizona and taking a few rests in between, it was midday when they felt a burning smell.

"What is this smell!" Marie exclaimed.

"I think it's the tires"

Sam parked the bike at the side of the road and upon investigating he found that their front tire is leaking air and in sometime will run flat.

"We'll need to call the highway services" Sam grumbled.

"I told you to take the other ROAD!!"

"Well women are indeed impulsive (laughs) does your phone havc a signal?"

"NO"

"Easy there, mine is also dead, we will have to find another way"

“Yeah Sherlock, I didn’t think of that, let’s stroll ahead for a bit I am sure our phones will pick up some network”

(Two days later)

“Hey guys have you read the newspaper today; we’ve got to cancel our trip, the situation is quite serious!!” Amanda exclaimed.

“Easy easy, it’s my house; mom doesn’t know about the trip whatsoever, keep calm” Jaden spoke quietly.

“What’s the news though? (laughs)” Ian shouted looking at Jaden who in return looked down.

“It’s not funny Ian, a couple of days ago two dead bodies have been found on the river bed in Arizona, I think we should postpone” Amanda said in a serious tone.

“We can’t do that, you were the one so excited for it; and it’s Marcella’s plan if she even gets a hint of the word that you want to cancel she will literally kill you, this is not a big deal come on just a two-day campaign” Ian resisted.

“The woman’s internal organs were found missing explain this ‘not a big deal’ guy” Amanda quarreled.

“I don’t know about that probably an animal, see I get this you are frightened, but all four of us have planned something after such a long time, it’s the call of the wind; just imagine us four campaigning in the wilderness of Arizona, you don’t get to spend time with Jaden nor me and Marcella nowadays, this is something that we’ve been planning for a long time, we must go”

Amanda looked at Jaden with seamless hope.

"We are going Amanda, what's there to fear anyways; I am with you, don't hesitate" Jaden said in a calm voice.

"Okay if you say so, but I am still not sure about this" Amanda hesitated a bit and hugged Jaden.

All of the four friends had completed their university education a couple of months ago, Jaden and Ian were childhood friends and the two girls got along from university, Marcella and Ian shared a common love for adventure, in their university days such expeditions were guided; this was the first time on their own.

The next day was the day of the trip, Jaden with his curly hair and brown leather jacket looked ready for the adventure as he sneaked out the house on his bike to pick up Amanda; Amanda looked stunning in her jeans and rugged top as she approached Jaden said.

"Giving complexion to the shining sun, I must say"

"You're getting better with flirting" Amanda said with a smile as she looked relieved from the chaos of the previous day.

"Let's get going"

Reaching the camping site was an eight-hour drive so they started early, they all first met at the freeway.

"It's a tough ride but we should fare just well, no pun intended" Ian laughed.

"Yes indeed, hello Marcella you missed the show yesterday" Jaden said with a smile.

“Which show?” Marcella asked looking at Ian.

“Let it go, Marcella, the boys have just lost it (laughs), let’s start we have to reach there before evening” Amanda said by nudging Jaden from the pillion seat of the bike.

“Yes indeed let’s get this trip ignited” Ian said by giving his bike acceleration like a phoenix raging through the clouds as Marcella grabbed his shoulder and saved herself from falling over.

Jaden followed him in a relatively subtler fashion on the void freeway.

The winds got dryer with each passing milestone, sun above their heads resembling a hot menace; deserted lands became a perpetual sight and patches of cactus could be seen from far and wide, high red mountains accompanied their journey with some occasional scream of eagles. At 1:45 P.M they reached the diversion and as Marcella narrated the nuances of each path, Amanda said.

“Let’s take the right one, it’s the shortest and we’ll reach the campsite earl....”

“OR, Ian and Marcella can take the right one; we’ll take the left and see who reaches the other side of this road first” Jaden suggested

“A tempting idea nonetheless!!, let’s do it” Ian exclaimed

“Whatever you say, as long as the destination is the same” Marcella nodded.

“Okay, so thank you Amanda for the approval, let’s go” Ian laughed

“Guys I don’t think this an idea to even consider, we should stay together" Amanda tried to convince

"And we will at the campsite, amazing idea bro, let's see whose bike has got what it takes" Ian jumped in excitement.

"Hey Amanda it's just a matter of some miles, it will be fun" Jaden said by looking at Amanda's eyes.

"You guys are just a sweet pain" Amanda said with a smile.

Both bikes were ready to run wild on the dry asphalt, as Amanda counted.

"3, 2, 1 GO!!"

And after the minutest of time differences only moving dust was evident where previously the bikes were, both of them throttled the accelerator to its maximum, and soon the only noises in the barren red lands were of loud engines.

Jaden and Amanda cruised through the dusty road taking glances at the high mountains above and the shallow river beneath until Jaden felt something.

"Do you smell something?" he asked

"Yes something is burning" Amanda replied

Jaden stopped the bike and watched his burnt tire.

"Probably it got punctured, can't move ahead like this, we'll have to call the highway service"

"I can't find any network here" Amanda said

Jaden looked all around in the deserted land and found a house in seclusion on the other side of the road, the house seemed to be more of an attic with a slanting wooden rooftop, cracked on some portions and huge windows on front walls closed with permanent shutters, a high windmill stood in the sandy courtyard with some cactus plants acting as guards around it.

"Who lives here?" Jaden murmured.

"No one, it's abandoned look the windows are closed so is the door, it's probably not in use since decades" Amanda said.

"Only one way to find out, let's go there"

"Hey, Jaden come on let's not do this we'll just stroll a bit and our phones will pick up network"

"Look at both the sides and not down the cliff, do you think we have any shot at finding something, maybe someone will help us ther....." Jaden said with the sounds of water gushing with the wind in background but was interrupted.

"Hey, there, lads can I help you somehow" a sound came from the direction in which the house was located.

Jaden turned to deduce the origin of the mysterious voice and saw a middle-aged man coming out of the feeble house cradling towards them with a stick in his hand, the man wore a black truckers cap, brown and white checkered shirt with ripped jeans of whose origin was time more than trend, unregulated white beard grew over his face with some empty patches.

"I heard some disturbing engine noises, just came to check; is everything alright" the old man asked in a deep sore voice.

“Yeah, actually the highway service would just be here in some time, we would leave in just a bit” Amanda said with a bit of haste trying to ignore him.

“They are never on time; believe me, and that is given that you found signal which I am surprised how you managed, but you can wait in my house I have a satellite phone which may come in handy for you, and yes I am Ralph, sorry for the late introduction”

“Thank you Ralph but I think we are just fine” Amanda hesitated as Ralph stared at her face as she spoke.

“I think we will use the phone Ralph..., if that’s not a problem?” Jaden asked with Ralph’s gaze turned at his face.

Ralph snapped out of his state and said.

“No, no absolutely not, visitors are scarce in this barren lands; I would like your presence to.... stay”

Ralph turned and started to walk to his house.

“I don’t need to be telling you this, we shouldn’t trust him” Amanda said to Jaden.

“I know but I don’t think we’ve got a choice, and he seems too fragile to carry his own stick, stay calm....”

“Hey, come on now” Ralph shouted from a bit far

“Yeah” Jaden replied.

Ralph went inside the house leaving the door open with Jaden and Amanda following him, as they were to enter the house Jaden saw an old car parked beside the house beneath a cracked shade, inside of the house was filled with rustic ambiance and relative darkness, no single object seemed whole midst the shadowy calmness of surreal silence, as they entered and sat on the wooden couch a scream came from behind.

"Macawwwwww!!"

Both of the wanderers looked back in utter shock moving away up from the couch.

(a lemur sprinted and jumped at Ralph's shoulder)

"Easy Boyce, don't worry lads he accompanies me here, I'll get some tea for you guys and please do not say no I insist really; seldom do I get visitors here" Ralph said to the visitors and turned toward the corridor which led to the kitchen.

"Let me help you" Jaden said by standing up from the couch Boyce screamed and Ralph turned to Jaden.

"You struggle not I will see to it, please be seated"

"As you say" Jaden said by sitting on the couch again.

"He lives with a lemur!!" Amanda exclaimed.

"He lives all alone in the middle of nowhere on clean energy (laughs)" nothing surprises me about him now Jaden replied.

"This place definitely needs some lights, I am surprised where all the windmill energy goes" Amanda said in amusement looking around the house and finding no lights but just some holes on the roof

"That's not our concern we will just call for highway service and be on our way"

"Looking forward to that"`

"Please don't put sugar in my tea Ralph, doesn't quite suit me!!" Jaden exclaimed toward the kitchen but no reply came just some sound of utensils tumbling.

"He's definitely a pro" Jaden laughed.

A few moments later Ralph came into the hall and handed separate tea cups in both their hands.

"You guys carry on I'll find the satellite phone in an instance" saying so Ralph moved toward the inside room.

"I am not drinking that" Amanda said.

"Sure you are not, let me have a sip"

Jaden lifted the thin tin cup and took a sip, just as he tasted some tea he spilled it back, he picked up the second cup and spilled it back in the cup after taking a sip saying

"I told him to abandon sugar, both cups have it, old age has taken over him maybe!" Jaden exclaimed.

After some time Ralph's lemur ran before Amanda and Jaden dashing out of the still-open front door.

"What happened to him?" Amanda said.

"Mr. Ralph what is taking you so long" Jaden shouted, but got no response.

“I will check it out” Jaden stood up and went toward the corridor leading to the other room.

“Stay sharp” Amanda said.

“He is just on the verge of getting old, what bad could possibly happen”

Jaden moved forward in the narrow wooden passage with his footsteps making creaking sounds on the floor below.

“Mr. Ralph, are you there” Jaden inquired.

As he made progress in the rustic corridor dodging from a broken glass chandelier hanging from the low roof, his leg fell on a trap door beneath, As Jaden looked down he saw the metal handle lifted, assuming that Ralph has gone down and probably the reason he is not hearing the voice Jaden decided to go there. He lifted the crooked door with its hinges showing vocal resistance and descended the wooden stairs until he reached its floor beneath, the wall toward the right side of the stairs converged into a corner after prolonging for a bit, Making slow progress to the corner of that wall Jaden got a glimpse of a bed on which he saw feet of a sleeping person, before Jaden could look any further his ears suddenly got shattered by a loud deafening noise and he fell to the ground covering ears, everything went white in front of his eyes, his limbs numb as frozen steel, eyes closed in search of hope, he rolled on the ground bashing his back to the wall, as he got a reckoning in his mind of his love sitting above, he gathered what was left in his body and tried to fight the riotous noise, crawling his way up the stairs and through the corridor banging his body back and forth at either side of the wooden corridor.

"Amanda, Amanda where are you?" He shouted midst the glaring noise.

He reached the hall and saw Amanda on the ground motionless with Ralph standing beside her with a wooden stick in his hand with his back facing toward Jaden.

"What have you done to her?" Jaden screamed, but Ralph gave no response.

It felt that the vociferous noise was not affecting Ralph at all, Jaden ran toward Ralph by picking up a vase from a table beside and pounded him on the head, rendering Ralph unconscious as he also fell to the ground.

Jaden tried to move Amanda but she barely showed resilience, he knew that the noise must be brought down first, Jaden lost power on his feet to stand up again and started to crawl to the room where Ralph went before, reaching there after a tough crawl he tried to find what has turned on this horrifying noise, he looked everywhere from the altitude he could and found an old metal switch beneath a broken dresser, he clung onto it and made the massacre stop by turning it down. Everything fell into singularity in just a movement, surreal silence shrouded the house and even minute sounds were easily distinguishable, Jaden stood up and went back to the hall struggling a bit on his feet, as he approached there he saw Amanda sitting on the floor resting her back on the couch, Jaden rushed to her and asked.

"Are you alright?, Amanda what did he do to you?"

"I was just sitting here when a thunderous noise struck me and I fell to the ground, then I saw Ralph approaching I tried to get up but couldn't, the noise was deafening; everything happened so fast,

Ralph came near me and smacked my head with a rod and I went totally blank"

Jaden embraced her in his arms and said

"There is no need to fear, love"

"Why would he do something like this?"

"That I don't know but maybe he is keeping something hidden, a hostage maybe in the dungeon beneath, we must see"

"WHAT!!"

"We must not leave Ralph like this, I think I saw a rope in the other room, I'll get it"

Jaden grabbed the rope and tied lifeless Ralph to the couch, after that both of them headed toward the dungeon beneath.

Moving beyond the corner this time Jaden saw an unconscious female resting on the bed connected to a ventilator, on it the dance of spikes and depths was evident, besides the bed was a refrigerator and upon opening it he saw some bottles of blood and some closed jars with perceived human organs, shaken by the sheer smell Jaden closed the door, Amanda pointed Jaden's focus toward a table on which several used surgical instruments resided, close to the bed were oxygen cylinders from which one was in work now, Looking closely to the woman on bed Jaden deduced that she was kept in a very grave condition, some portions of her body were not patched up, and some minute things like the beeping ventilator and a subtly moving torso were the only evidence of life in her.

"What could it be Jaden" Amanda asked in disbelief.

“I will not risk guessing it, only one man can explain.... Ralph”

“He is dangerous Jaden, the deafening noise, it had no effect on him, cannot trust that guy”

“He is deaf Amanda, yes he is, he didn’t hear the noise he produced, that’s why he couldn’t hear when I shouted to him, when I said I don’t want sugar, his lemur reflects to sound and taking the cue he responds, remember how he starred at us outside, maybe cause he was reading our lips”

“Indeed, but still be we have to be careful”

Both of them climbed the stairs and entered the hall, Ralph was already awake.

“WHAT DID YOU DO, where you were, tell me!!” Ralph exclaimed.

“See Ralph we know what you’ve hidden beneath, we also know you are deaf, crippled; tell me what are you up to, tell me WHAT have you done!!” Jaden said by going close to Ralph as he just looked down.

“Speak up Ralph!!” Jaden punched the couch.

“She.... she is my wife, I am just trying to keep her alive, that’s all”

“No you are not, not in this menacing lands and not with the torturing equipment I saw on the table below, she is not living here she is suffering”

“What are you talking about” Ralph said in a sobbing voice.

“Amanda take her off the ventilator and call the emergency they’ll see what to do with him and save her"

"NO, No you must not disconnect the ventilator it would kill her in an instance, don't let her die please don't let her die she must live, she must live here with me, she cannot die, I will tell you the truth please don't let her die" Ralph said with his face reflecting utter grief.

"Then tell us what happened"

"Jus.... just like you both, were me and Scarlet my wife; happy, joyous she liked adventures it was a part of her life as she.... she said, after 4 months of friendship we got married everything happened as fast as I can now remember, it was perfect, I was madly in love with her, after two months of our wedding she wanted to come here for campaign; at first I resisted but then I.... as I loved her I agreed for the travel, 7 years ago we came here drenched in love, we went ahead from this place and we reached where the two diverted paths converged, there we saw an old lean man asking for a lift, I neglected as we were on a bike but Scarlet stopped me to help him, asking the old man he said, that he just wanted to go half a mile ahead where his people are waiting for him, Scarlet said that she would stay back until I fare off the old man and come back to pick her up, it was just half a mile of tour so I agreed, but who would have thought that would change the course of my life, as I dropped off the old man some tribal people surrounded me; the old man got lost between them, before I could have done anything they took me to their place, I was in complete shock as to what has happened; they tortured me for days they said they are preparing me for sacrifice a ritual, I was broken, my ability to hear got stolen from me, they crippled me and did horrified things that are painful to even imagine, but everyday I thought of Scarlet as to what would have happened to her and then one day I saw....."

"You saw what?" Jaden asked.

"It was her, she was part of the same cult which had tortured me in unprecedented ways, she looked at me tied to a wooden pole as she smiled at my face, I still remember that smile, I never wanted to get out of there more, one night I found my opportunity, I robbed a cultist of a knife and tried to run from the place it was hard as I had suffered many injuries but the thought of redemption was what propelled me (smiles) Scarlet was also there, I knocked her as she slept, stole a car from their warren and took her here at this place where not many people came regularly, a perfect lair sufficient of what I wanted to do, I cuffed her up until this place was ready for the inevitable, I was a doctor.... once, it helped me, I cuffed her to the bed beneath as my redemption found it's aim, I created the noises you heard, I would play that for the whole day, I couldn't hear anything nor her scream but the very sight of her suffering made me satisfied, I tortured her in every way that they had seeded in my imagination, but her body began to gave up after some time.... I couldn't let that happen, she could never die after what she did to me she HAS to suffer still"

"YOU are mad!!" Amanda exclaimed as Ralph laughed.

"Mad is an understatement" Jaden said.

"Wait, it must be you who killed the two people who came here some days ago"

"NO, No.... not just them (laughs), Scarlet's organs were giving up on her, every now and then sometimes she needs a donor, she needs blood and the visitors certainly helped, I've rigged these roads, Boyce signals their arrival and then the noises play their part, my love is sleeping now, the last surgery was certainly a work of art, remind me to turn on the noises when she gains consciousness (laughs)" Ralph said to Jaden with a subtle laugh as he concluded.

Jaden and Amanda both were taken aback by the sheer cruelty of this evident reality, Jaden said.

"We must try to save her, cannot leave her like this, there must be keys to his car parked outside, search around"

Looking above Amanda found a bunch of keys hanging on the antlers of a deer's head on the wall.

"There it is!" Amanda pointed.

"Very well you take the car, go to the police call the medics I will stay here and watch this maniac" Jaden said.

"No, I am not going anywhere without you"

"You have to, we have no other choice, can't leave him alone here, now go and be quick"

Amanda turned and went toward the open door as Jaden followed her, just as Amanda was going outside Jaden received a harsh push from behind, he fell to the ground taking Amanda with him, as he reconciled and looked behind he saw Ralph trying to run toward the dungeon, his gaze also caught Boyce running to the kitchen as his mind cleared the uncertainty.

Jaden got back up on his feet and ran after Ralph, Amanda followed, when they both reached down they saw Ralph holding a surgical knife to Scarlet's throat murmuring to himself.

"You cannot live again.... no, you must stay here with me"

The faint shadow of Jaden caught Ralph's attention as he turned around without moving the knife in his hand, he shouted

"She cannot live again she is mine to suffer!!!!"

"Drop the knife Ralph let her go" Jaden exclaimed.

But it was too late, Ralph gutted the knife through Scarlet's throat and Scarlet for once showed real signs of life as her soul left her body, Jaden tried to come forward as Ralph said.

"Bye-bye lads, you cannot separate us"

Ralph took the knife to his throat and pierced himself with a smile on his face, Jaden and Amanda rushed forward to the two fallen lifeless bodies and concluded them dead, Amanda ruptured into tears seeing the very sight of gore, Jaden consolidated her with a tight hug, just a few moments later Jaden remembered.

"Amanda we have to get to Ian and Marcella, remember what Ralph said that the cultists reside where the two roads converge, we must get to them"

Both ran to the car outside and Jaden throttled it as tough as he could, trying to reach his friends.

"See we reached first, Jaden doesn't like losing he would be upset" Ian laughed as he reached at the point where the roads converged.

"Yes certainly" Marcella affirmed.

Just as they both were waiting for their friends an old man approached them and said.

"Can you give me a lift young man, my destination is just a mile ahead and I can barely walk that much"

"Sorry pal, this bike won't take three can't leave her behind in this place, perhaps some other time...."

"Oh, shut up Ian I'll be just fine it's just a matter of a mile, come back to pick me up" Marcella spoke with a faint smile.

CHAPTER THREE

IMMORTAL LOVE

It was a serene night with snowfall blurring the evidence of the moon shining through the wooden framed windows on the 9th floor of his apartment when he heard the knocking on the door; he stopped reading and went to respond.

"The weather of Alaska does not seem to be your friend" the woman at the door exclaimed.

"But certainly you are, welcome Jessica" Abraham and Jessica shared a hug.

Jessica came in and removed her trench coat putting it on the table.

"You still keep a gun Jess" Abraham said as he saw the holster on Jessica's waist.

"Yes for safety from guys like you and bears" Jessica said with a huge laughter.

They both sat on lounges facing each other beside the fireplace and talked for a couple of hours and suddenly interrupting Abraham midst the sentence Jessica asked cautiously

"How has it really been?"

“I told you everything is just fine” Abraham replied with a bit of pause

“You keep telling yourself that, like that is what you really feel, four years have passed you haven’t met your parents living secluded here working relentlessly, look at this place, is this what you really want”

“For now; yes, you know I can’t go back”

“Stop addressing your priorities as facts!!” Jessica exclaimed.

“Easy friend, I’ll do something about it” Abraham said with a calm yet guilty voice.

“I know you won’t that is why I have something for you, if you don’t want to go back that’s your decision, but you are certainly going to climb Mount Agape”

Abraham’s eyes enlarged wide with sheer joy as he asked Jessica.

“Really that’s wonderful, how did you get the permissions though?”

“Just stick to your business; I knew this was the only thing that could give you a breather”

“I know that there’s no point to ask, but can’t you come along” Abraham asked

“Would love to if the mountain wasn’t this high (laughs), you know I don’t fare nicely with heights; and also I am going to my parents house as well, for some days so I won’t be here, you are alone in your love for adventure boy” Jessica replied with a smile

Abraham's eyes fell down to his toes and realizing that he looked up and said in a depreciated tone

"If you could have came along, it would have been better"

"If I could I would have surely come, you'll just be fine, believe me I know you since like holocaust" Jessica said with a laugh.

"Yeah you make your jokes Jess, but as you say"

"Just be a bit careful I've heard some weird stories about that place"

"So have I, don't worry you know I got my research covered"

"Then see you on your return mate, have a nice hike" Jessica concluded with a subtle smile.

Mount Agape was a snow-covered mountain with marginal hikers going that way for the risks and stories it possessed, it was a one-day hike if everything followed according to the plan.

The day of the hike arrived with Abraham reaching the base early in his shallow white jacket and violet tinted eyeglasses, his long hairs flew with the wind escaping his cap, he stood tall looking at the summit in glaring fashion, when an old official came to ask for permission papers to hike.

"Papers please" the old man asked?

Abraham handed them over and marveled.

"Isn't it beautiful!"

"And dangerous, especially in this weather, but it has it's perks" the old man said while looking at the papers.

“Perks?” Abraham asked with eagerness.

“Perhaps your research is based on internet only, folk lore says....”

“Stop right there old man, I am not so much for lore’s and all but thanks”

“Whatever suits you have a nice hike, if you don’t return in two days we will begin the search operation”

“You’ve got it” Abraham said and marched towards the mountain.

Weather was a bit gloomy and even at midday, there were only subtle sign of sun rays, as Abraham strolled between the sky reaching trees and their hushing noises. The hike was fairly steep after he crossed halfway and foot long snow didn’t did any favors so he decided to take a halt resting his back on the bark of a storm fallen tree, he took out Jessica’s photo from his bag and then talked to himself.

“Hey beautiful, it has been a long time since we are friends together but I feel something more for you, I just haven’t had the courage to tell but...., perhaps at a suitable time..”

A swift noise passed at some distance from Abraham, he looked around but found no one in the little what he could see, after a pause he heard sounds of some Alaskan moose and concluded likewise, then he slid the photo back in the bag and moved forward.

It was afternoon now, with Abraham reaching close to the summit but his strides were stopped by an ice wall standing straight on rocky grounds, he knew that there were chances of this hike being converted to a climb in this season, he came prepared, taking out his ice hammers he began to climb the frozen wall of fragile ice.

Abraham was a swift climber and had accomplished many climbs like this but this weather was not getting easy on him, winds made him struggle more than lack of visibility, he was gaining height but the progress was slow, he had conquered more than half the climb and something drastic happened of which he did not anticipate, his attempt to peck the hammer in thin ice was bundled as that patch of ice let loose on him, he saw cracks being developed with creaking sound around the other ice hammer as he knew something needed to be done in urgent fashion, but before he made any further deductions ice supporting his shoes ruptured and now he was hanging with the only support of one hammer on cracked ice which soon released his hand from the struggle of carrying his whole weight sending Abraham into free fall midst the silent ambience of hustling tress, he fell foot first on some snowy rocks but was still conscious to see some slabs of ice falling before him, of which one fell on his right leg with its sharp edges tearing through tissues and pardoning bones, soon he felt his eyes craving for a shade of light in whatever he could barely see but he quickly knew complete darkness as his lids closed, rendering him helpless between towering trees and wintry snow.

Everything was slowly becoming clear from abstract blurriness while a barking dog distracted him, he rubbed his eyes to see better in lying position but that didn't help him as he heard a voice with great depth.

"You're awake finally"

Abraham tried seeing who spoke and could only deduce a man sitting with his back toward him, he tried to move but his legs showed minimal response, he asked out of fear.

"Who are you?, where am I?"

"You have nothing to worry about friend, relax with this soothing winds, they will help you get better"

Abraham tried to see where he was but could only capture blurred snapshots of a rocky cave with wood fire at some places; the place was soothingly warm, seeing Abraham try to sit, the dog rush toward the man, the man said.

"Hey Bruno, he won't harm you, do not worry"

As Abraham managed to be seated on the wooden bench things became more blurred for a second and suddenly everything was clear, he saw his right leg was bandaged with tree branches and bark fibers, his bag was rested alongside his bench, he saw the man making something on his table which was lighted by a firewall torch, the old man spun the wheels of his chair with one hand, holding a cup in another and moved toward the wooden bench, as Abraham saw him approaching on his wheelchair the old man's face became clear, he had a long white beard, a red woollen scarf around his head, his brows were withered beneath which eyes spoke with intensity, he had a worn-out brown jacket on his lean body with padded trousers on his quiet legs, as he came close enough he said by offering the cup.

"Take this it will help you recover"

Abraham took the cup and asked out of astonishment.

"Who are you?"

"Your friend" The man replied with a smile.

Abraham looked at the eyes of the man and drank soup from the cup cautiously.

"Be relieved, there are not many reasons to first wake you up and then kill you with a hot soup" the man spoke with a smile.

"What is this place?" Abraham asked expecting an answer

"This is where I live with Bruno as you can see, he was the one who found you passed out over the ridge, see those tearing marks on your jacket, Bruno pulled you till here, he is a good boy"

"How bad is my leg?"

"It is not in the best condition but there isn't much to worry about (after a brief pause) you'll walk sooner" the man replied with a bit of grief in his voice.

"That's good to hear, do you live here alone?" Abraham asked with a cautioned accent.

"No, it's hard for a person with no legs to roam in this wilderness (laughs) I live with Bruno as I told and there is also my daughter who lives atop the mountain"

"Sorry, your daughter?" Abraham asked in amusement

"Yes she lives there alone, dose not come down often or talk to me, (looking at his legs) and I can't go up there, when you reach the top and see her tell that I love her more than anything else, would you do that for me, please?" The man replied by turning his wheelchair around with tears in his eyes.

"Yes sure, why not, shall I ask why she does not stay with you?" Abraham asked with a calm voice.

The man turned his wheelchair and answered.

"Time has been cruel to us in the past and still to say the least, I had a glittering family my wife Amanda, me, Bruno and Bella our 17 year old daughter she loved our family more than any of us, we were fond to go on hikes and treks Bella was most excited about such adventures, Do you know what Agape means, it's the purest form of love that exist between people, in ancient times this mountain was the symbol of love, inspired by this five years ago Bella planned to come here particularly in this winter season she said that this would strengthen our bond as a family, Amanda and I wanted to postpone a bit but not her, Bella was too thrilled by lore's which accompanied this place....."

"Which lore?" Abraham asked impulsively

"It is said that whoever makes a wish at the top of this mountain in this season for their loved ones must come to pass but a sacrifice must be provided which is the life of a living, I didn't believed in that, Bella did and Amanda too till an extent, so we started the hike, Bruno was also with us, it was evening when we came to a place which is beneath us right now, ambience was just like today, to reach the summit we had some tough hiking to do, so we decided to take some rest first on that open plateau, Bella had a tendency to go ahead on hikes and leave directions behind on a piece of paper for us to follow, she did the same that day and took Bruno with her, after having a meal me and Amanda sat on the edge of the ridge looking far into the wilderness, I still remember when I said,

"What a beautiful spectacle this is"

And she replied.

"Even if I could live long enough to see every beautiful sight in this world I would still watch you till my last breath" (tears ran down the man's face).

Time passed quickly then ever, we were lost in the serene beauty of what was before us as Amanda said breaking the silence that Bella must have reached the top leaving the markings behind we should go now just when we stood up a thundering noise came from behind like the one we had never heard till that date, it was the sound of an avalanche it came out of nowhere, everything happened in blink of an eye there was chaos everywhere tons of snow came rushing toward us, midst that trembling Amanda's leg slipped off the ridge and I grabbed her by the wrist with his whole body hanging below, I laid flat on snow with my hand grabbing onto Amanda's wrist as tight as it could in that time I heard Bella's cry for help, I turned to see just when a tree fell with a thud on both my legs, Amanda's wrist slipped from hand and my disbelief continued, but somehow I gathered myself, there was still someone who needed my help, I dug myself out of snow with hands but my eyes were closed soon, when I woke up I was in this cave on this wheel chair with Bruno besides me and as I opened my eyes Bella ran toward the summit I tried to follow but the wheels stopped me" the man concluded with wiping off his tears with hand.

"Why is Bella so mad at you?"

"You must ask her that yourself, see the sun is rising you must go to witness the spectacle the cliff holds, your leg shouldn't be much of a hindrance now"

"As you say, see you on my way down" Abraham wobbled a few strides and then began to set in.

"Perhaps...." the old man grumbled with a soft voice.

Abraham reached the top after a hard time with his leg, and the beauty he saw there astonished him, clouds filtered the soothing sun rays which energized him and winds ran through his long hairs, he gazed around to find a sight of a woman but could find none, till he heard a weeping sound from behind a rock.

“Who’s there!” Abraham exclaimed.

A woman came out from behind, her face was drenched in agony she was wearing a black dress with her hair open, her eyes were surrounded by black circles and her skin was whitish pink.

“Who are you?” Abraham asked again.

"I’d heard that the mountain grants every wish, it’s really true" the woman spoke in a pitch-less accent.

“Look Bella, just tell me what’s wrong” Abraham exclaimed.

“Bella, where is she, where is she, tell me” the woman asked in an urgent fashion.

“You’re not Bella, who are you”

“I am Amanda her mother, how do you know Bella tell me now”

Everything fell into singularity for Abraham as he said to himself.

“This cant be, this can’t be”

“What, HOW YOU KNOW BELLA” the woman shouted.

“Her dad told me that she would be here and I must bring her down to him” Abraham replied in a nervous voice.

“You’re lying; it’s been five years since my husband died”

“I just MET him a while ago he healed me” Abraham spoke in disbelief.

"He died in an avalanche five years ago; my whole family did only I survived"

"How did you survive the avalanche" Abraham asked by slowly stepping back.

"I fell from a ridge as my hand slipped from my husband's palm, the deep snow acted as a cushion just enough to keep me alive until the paramedics arrived and I was saved, in the hospital I received news that my husband was found far from the ridge trying to move up the cliff by dragging his body without legs but died in a cave with paper cutouts in his hand on which directions were drawn" Amanda said with tears in her eyes.

"What happened to your daughter?"

"Her body was found at the top of mountain just here, she was found dead with a letter in her hand which said 'I make this wish that me and my family would stay together forever and ever till the dawn of time', and there is only one way that could occur, outside of this perishing body as immortal souls, she sacrificed our dog Bruno and killed him with her own hands before killing herself"

"She must be mad, who does this"

"In love yes, she believed that it could work and it did until they took my body off the mountain and the wish was unfulfilled, it needed me to be here, I was paralyzed from taking the fall, my mind and body numb from outside, until four days ago I was revitalized, I knew I had to complete the wish"

"You're mad, nothing like this exists, I know you love your family a lot, live off their memories, what are you doing!!"

“Memories are only as good as you remember them to be, intangible, sometimes even perfect which blurs the original aspects, I want to be again with my family and for that I’ll have to revive the wish again”

“And how you plan on doing that”

“By making another sacrifice” Amanda said by pulling a gun out of her black dress and pointing it toward Abraham.

“Don’t do this, nothing of what you believe is true!!”

“You’ve seen my husband haven’t you? it just means that the wish is indeed true”

“He is not like you, he thinks he is guilty of your death”

“He was always a bit aloof from me and Bella and didn’t knew about this, but will certainly understand why we did what we did, Bella thinks her dad is the reason the wish didn’t work out as he let me go but she’ll come around as well, after all a healthy family has a bit of sour feelings”

“You’re literally mad, you brainwashed your daughter into killing entire family”

"She wanted the same thing; you wouldn’t understand doesn’t need to actually" Amanda said.

Amanda’s finger moved toward the trigger and a gunshot was heard, a few seconds later Amanda fell on the ground, Abraham checked as he was okay he looked sideways and saw Jessica standing with a gun in her hand which shot Amanda’s head, Abraham’s eyes were filled with tears of joy as he ran with a fragile foot and embraced Jessica.

“You really thought I was going to let you come here alone, I wanted to surprise you”

“You’re the sweetest Jess, I can explain everything but first I wanted to tell you something” Abraham said with a smile.

“No I just killed someone I’ll go first” Jessica giggled in Abraham’s arms.

“Okay say”

“I love you Abraham, and I wish that we stay together FOREVER AND EVER”.

CHAPTER FOUR

EMMA CREED

"Hey, you off to work early today?" Erik surprisingly asked.

"Yeah, client wants to see this new house at Wisconsin, out of the blue" Emma replied while putting things in her bag.

"4 years since we have married and one thing I can say for sure, you have the perkiest clients" Erik laughed.

"Make all the jokes you want; I won't be home until two weeks"

"As you say miss...."

Emma's phone rang, Erik took a look at the caller which spelled `Poseidon`.

"It's your client again...."

"Coming" Emma picked up the phone from the table and kissed Erik goodbye; rushing out of the door.

It was the other end of the city, Emma's car entered a lavish villa whose driveway was paved with cobbled stone, fountains covered garden on both the sides, she handed the keys to the valet and entered the atrium.

“What took you this long!, love.” Amiraz exclaimed, rushing down the spiral staircase.

“You know my work can take time to converge” Emma answered.

“That is indeed the harsh reality” Amiraz rushed down the stairs and hugged Emma.

“You know you don’t need to work right?” Amiraz said.

“We have been down this road before....” Emma whispered.

“Master Amiraz, there is an urgent call for you” Butler interrupted.

“It can wait”

“You won’t change will you” Emma stepped back and asked.

“Not until you are this beautiful” Amiraz smiled.

“Where I am today is because of you, I don’t think you are given enough credit for that” Emma said by smiling back.

"Sure you are, beautiful" Amiraz sported an intense smile and offered a dink to her.

“Ah, you always know what I want” Emma said.

“So how is the work forming up in travel industry” Amiraz asked.

“Like it has been, today here tomorrow there”

“Just the life you wanted, my mother also wants something”

“What?”

“You know that pretty well, a successor to inherit the estate, the family name”

“We have talked about this before...”

“I know, but what I don’t; is for how long will I be able to handle her, you must understand, but I can take care of her for sometime”

“You know me very well”

“I do, so what is the plan this time, our anniversary is coming, this time let’s celebrate together”

“You know I want to....”

“Then it’s settled, I know you don’t like public appearances, it will just be a small glitter with some family members, so we are having the celebration next Monday”

“But try to hear me out....”

“What I said, stands, see you my love, got to leave now” saying this Amiraz left the villa.

As soon as Amiraz left, Emma rushed to her room and called Erik.

“Hey, honey are you free now?” Emma asked.

“Well the stocks are steady so yes, is everything okay? Erik asked.

“Yes, just wanted to update you that I won’t be able to return before the month end as there are some additional estates the client need to ponder upon”

"Okay, no worries, you know I will always support you"

"You are the best honey, see you"

"Thank you Love, bye"

The day of celebration arrived, there was a small gathering of family members in the villa, huge chandeliers covered the high ceilings, with red carpets stretched midst the floors, Amiraz and Emma both sat on the podium watching the proceedings.

"I have always dreamt of celebrating our anniversary together for the 3 years we have been together..."

"And tonight it has been realized"

Emma's phone on the table ranged with a sting and Amiraz being near to it saw the name which spelled "Hades"

"Ah, your boss doesn't let you breath much does he"

"Maybe he has learnt from you" Emma replied with a smile.

"You can take that, if you want"

"Umm, no that can wait (she declined the call), but I will have to leave tomorrow"

"I understand"

"Thank you for always doing"

It was a snowy night at the stadium in Utah where a match of the American premier league was underway, both the teams were level at half time and as the players receded to the dressing room Diaz saw Emma in the crowd, he looked down and continued his walk, the play resumed but Diaz's team lost in the final minutes, after the game Emma rushed to the lobby and met Diaz.

"Have you came to mock me for the loss?" Diaz asked seeing Emma.

"Don't talk like you mean it Diaz" Emma said with tears pouring from her eyes.

"You were supposed to be here 2 days before"

"I am really sorr..."

Before Emma could finish the sentence Diaz launched his hand and slapped Emma, rendering her to the ground.

"Don't do this Diaz" Emma said in a sobbing voice.

"You know I don't mean to" Diaz's voice found calmness and he helped Emma up.

"Forgive me Emma you know how it is with me, I am sorry"

Emma didn't answered as she got up.

"I have a surprise planned for you at home; actually it is from two days ago but..., let's go home now"

After reaching home as soon as Emma opened the door, Diaz's mother Karen popped up the party poppers and lit all the lights in the hall, and a cake was evident.

"Welcome dear, my eyes were scorching for you" Karen said and hugged Emma, as she looked at the red spot on her chicks, she said.

"Diaz, how my times I have told you to not hurt Emma, when will you understand"

"Yes mother, I do realize" Diaz said.

After cutting the cake all of them sat for dinner.

"Emma I know that things have not been the best between us two for sometime, and I think I know the reason too" Diaz said.

"What would be that dear?" Emma asked.

"A child, it will really help bring the family together, and after two years of marriage I think it's time.

"I don't know if I am ready Diaz"

"Take your time, there's no need to rush"

"And she wouldn't rush!" Karen exclaimed.

"I know your expeditions don't help the marriage much, but you too must keep it together" Karen said.

"We will mother, we will" Diaz said.

That night Emma was alone in the room, she opened the door to the bathroom and stood before the pale mirror, she started to cut down her long shiny hairs with a blunt scissor.

"You are not ready for this" Emma whispered to herself.

"YOU are not ready for this" she whispered in an angry accent.

“A child was never the part of this game, it’s all changing now”

“This isn`t the time” Emma`s voice found solace.

It had been two months since Emma left Utah, there was no sign of her, but then Erik, Amiraz and Diaz received a voicemail.

“I loved you too much to let you know in person at least for now, Tomorrow I have a surprise for you at the same place we got married, don’t worry I know your schedule, you are free”.

Erik got there as early as he could in the morning, he looked for traces of Emma but couldn’t find her, instead his eyes fell on a person who was looking for someone, he was Amiraz.

“Hey you looking for someone?" Erik asked.

“Yes, my wife actually, her name is Emma, stunningly beautiful, long hair....” Amiraz tried to explain.

“Since how long is she missing?" Erik asked by interrupting.

“Around two months, yesterday got a voice mail from her, to meet at this place, where we got married”.

A million questions squandered in Erik’s mind as he tried to make sense of any of this, just when both of them heard a voice from behind.

“Hey, gentleman, I am looking for someone, have you guys seen my wife, been looking for her since last two months, her name is Emma”

“Is she your wife, Amiraz asked in amusement”

"Yes, she left me two months ago, maybe I was a little too harsh on her"

Erik took a photo out from his wallet and showed it to both of them, is this the Emma you all are talking about.

"YES" both of them answered in amusement.

"She is my wife, atleast that's what I believed"

"WHAT?, I don't understand any of this!" Diaz exclaimed.

"Where did you two got married on this Island`` Amiraz asked Erik and Diaz,

"At the church behind that hill" Erik pointed.

"This can't be true we got married there" Diaz said in astonishment.

"Me too, perhaps that is the place we must visit again" Amiraz said.

All three of them entered the church in disbelief, at the altar they saw the father standing with his back toward them.

"Hey, father, have you seen here a woman, here name is Emma" Erik shouted.

"She said you all would visit" the father said by turning around.

"She told me to give this to you" The father handed a piece of paper to them and went for penance.

Amiraz opened the letter and began to read out loud.

"I know a million questions would be running around your fragile yet beautiful minds, but you must calm down. I know this won't be easy, but it was neither for me, you all loved me for who I am, but you will be happy to know that wasn't the real me, my full real name is Emma creed, I am a physiologist, studying human brains is what I live for, and for that today I must leave you all, It has been difficult to cope up lately, and I am not ready for what comes next, not now, for that I must be gone, I know none of you will try to find me, because you all know that you wont be able to, Thank you for all the things you have helped me learn – Emma Creed".

Diaz kicked the wooden bench in the silent church and hurt himself, Amiraz tried to keep his cool and called his assets to search for Emma, as Erik visualized and said.

"It all, makes perfect sense (Amiraz and Diaz both looked at him), we three have totally different personalities, backgrounds; we were just like lab rats for her.

"She can't go away like this, I won't let her" Diaz shouted.

"Too bad she isn't here to hear that" Erik smiled and walked out of the church, after a while Amiraz and Diaz also left the atrium.

Time flew with an effect lame, memories of Emma still persisted in all of the shattered hearts, Alas 7 years had passed now, Erik took to the profession of a writer and travel blogger, he visited many countries around the world and once he decided to visit Barcelona in Spain.

It was a busy day, there was quite a hustle on the streets, everyone going about their daily chores, passing through the busy market Erik's eyes stumbled upon a breathing beauty, he thought he had seen Emma, but before he can deduce she vanished in the crowd, Erik tried to look around to find a glimpse and he did, it was Emma wearing a sun hat with bags of fruits in her hand walking along the pathway, Erik decided to follow her.

Every step Erik took increased curiosity in his mind and pain in his crumbled heart, soon Emma entered a house, Erik was in dilemma of what to do now, he made up his mind and knocked on the wooden door, Emma opened the door and what she saw baffled her, her ever sparkling eyes went numb for a bit. Erik gazed at her in amusement and said with a smile.

"Long time"

"How did you find me? Erik"

"I never tried to...."

"Who is it Emma" a man asked from within the house.

"Just an old friend" Emma replied.

"What is he doing outside, invite him over"

"I am not here to fight Emma" Erik said.

"Hey pal come on in, not many of her friends I get to meet" A man came from behind Emma and said.

Erik entered the house and sat on the couch.

"He is Erik, a friend from when I lived in USA" Emma spoke.

"Ah, nice to meet you Erik, I am Marco Emma's husband, we have been married for four years"

"Ah, interesting" Erik nodded.

“Its been long since we met Erik” Emma said.

“Indeed that is the case” Erik replied.

“Emma we have the whole day to talk, bring some tea for the guest”

Emma went in the kitchen.

“It’s a pity our kids aren’t at home, you would have been glad to meet them”

“Is it so, I guess we will have to wait for that” Erik replied.

“I can actually show you some beautiful images of them which Emma regularly clicks”

Marco got up and tried to find Emma’s phone but couldn’t.

“Emma couldn’t find your phone, remember where you put it” Marco asked in a loud voice so Emma can hear in the kitchen.

“No I can’t, will search for you when I come outside” Emma answered.

“Ah, I won’t wait for that, hey Erik hear for a ring I am calling to Emma’s phone”

“Sure” Erik affirmed.

Marco took out his phone and dialed Emma`s cell, the ring surfaced from within the hall, Erik realized he was sitting on top of it, he moved and took Emma`s phone in his hand, before giving it to Marco he saw the caller name which was ‘Zeus’.

CHAPTER FIVE

ALONE AND ALONG

(22-Nov 09:45 PM)

Winter had started to fade now, as the shining sun started to peek above the pacified horizon just when an ominous dusk awaited Sinha's residence in Mumbai. Vihaan was a project manager at an IT firm just returning from his work upon entering his house he saw his better half sitting on the couch with repulsion in her eyes.

"I have been calling you since long Vihaan, where were you" Ahana asked.

"Was busy with some work, really sorry; and yes I will be out tonight Ahana, colleagues are insisting and I must go" Vihaan said (she skipped a reply)

Moments passed and Ahana stayed glued to where she sat, Vihaan got dressed up and was ready to leave.

"See you tomorrow honey" Vihaan said while opening the front door.

"Why?" Ahana murmured in a soft voice.

"What, you said something honey?" Vihaan asked by turning back.

“It has been 3 years since our marriage and 3 years since we haven’t spent quality time together, gone out somewhere.... just be together, you don’t have time for me, you never have” Ahana said with a sobbing tone.

“Not again Ahana, and certainly not now, I am getting late, we will talk about this some other time” Vihaan said.

“There is never another time with you”

“It’s not like that”

“I will go by myself If I have to, sometimes I wonder what compelled you to get married, if that is not what you wanted”

“You know that is not true”

“I feel like I know nothing, not even you” Ahana stood up and went to the bedroom.

Vihaan looked down and went outside the house.

(23 Nov 4:50 AM)

Darkness had squandered over the busy streets of Mumbai, only an occasional chirp of cricket broke the silence, Vihaan opened the door and came inside his house, he saw Ahana sitting still on the couch, as he made progress towards her, she said

“What have you made of yourself, why are your clothes all worn out?” Ahana asked

“Let that go Ahana, get ready we are going on a road trip today”

Vihaan replied

"Are you serious, just give me a second I will gather my things, where are we going?" Ahana's face glittered with joy and exhilaration

“Does it matter until we are together” Vihaan looked into her eyes and smiled.

Both of them embarked on the car and started the journey along the mountains of Pune highway, the soothing rays of warm sun just did enough to balance out the cold breeze of winter mornings, radiance of the surreal atmosphere was only met by Vihaan and Ahana looking at each other as if time was unreal.

After moving around all day exploring forts, evening knocked on the skies and Ahana decided to take a bit of a breather, at the side of the highway there was a vendor selling masala cucumbers which she loved, Ahana went to the other side of the road to get those while Vihaan parked the car facing the cliff's drop below; he rested his back on the car's bonnet and looked back at the sight to behold; her wife. Ahana returned with the raw delicacies, she offered Vihaan but he refused, both of them just stared at each other for a while and then stimulated their glances at nature's beauty, After a time lost in memories Ahana hugged Vihaan saying.

“We should do this more often”

Vihaan's lifted his arms and hugged her back, closing his eyes, he said

“Surely we should”

As he opened his eyes, there was nothing in his arms except thin volatile air, and tears started running down his cheek.

(23-Nov 3:00 AM)

Vihaan was busy partying at his friend's house as he received a call.

"Hello, am I speaking to Mr. Vihaan" the caller asked.

"Yes you are" Vihaan said by moving away from the loud noise.

"We have a patient just admitted named Ahana Sinha, got your number from her mobile she had last called you...."

"She is my wife, WHERE is she now, HOW is she?" Vihaan exclaimed.

"At the city hospital, she met an accident, her condition is not good"

"I am coming"

Vihaan dropped the phone and raced in his car to the hospital.

"Where is Ahana.... Ahana Sinha, she just got admitted here" Vihaan exclaimed at the front desk.

The attendant guided him to the ICU ward where he wasn't allowed to enter, he did manage to get a glance inside from the big glass on the wall, what he saw broke him, Ahana was laying on the bed with medical equipment and doctors all around her, Vihaan eyes stared though the plain glass; helpless. After a moment seeing the doctor come out Vihaan asked with fading hope.

"I am her husband, how is she, sh.. she will recover right?

"She was in a bad condition when she got here, her car crashed into a tree while she was driving at ferocious speeds on the ill lit highway, we tried but failed to save her, she is no more, I am sorry" Saying this the doctor walked away.

Hearing this Vihaan sat on the steel bench outside the ward, and soon got in his car and rushed home.

CHAPTER SIX

ABHAY AND THE MARKET OF MIDLIFE

It was the night before his 30th birthday, Abhay was exhausted after returning from a tiring day at work, he threw the laptop bag on the couch and went straight to the bed, he was so exhausted he didn't care to switch off all the lights, he wished for no one to wake him up at midnight to wish, as he was in no place to respond, his eyes dwindled into the verse of darkness and soon at midnight he woke up.

As he opened his eyes all he saw were blinding lights, he stood up and tried to analyze, where was he. The first thing he noticed was he wasn't tired anymore, he was fully rejuvenated, he cared to look for anyone around but couldn't find a personality in sight. All of a sudden a hand came from behind followed by a deep with a deep voice.

"You are welcome here, Abhay"

Abhay turned around in astonishment, what he saw was a man standing wearing a brown tethered robe, with his face covered by a hood of similar fashion, Abhay asked.

"Who are you? what is this place?"

"I am but a guide, for a place this is, a market seeking out people in their midlife who look to gain for in exchange of something that they already possess" the man in the robe answered.

"I don't understand what you mean by that"

"You soon will, come with me"

Both of them walked for a bit in a place where there was nothing but brightness, after a bit they reached the entrance.

"This is a place very simple, you have just what you came with in here, trade it for the things you like in return, once you leave this place you will get all the things you traded for, In the outside world you are still sleeping, a dream is what you can consider this, except what you do stays forever, you will again find me here once you return" saying this the man in the robe vanished.

Abhay was still in utter shock, he tried to pinch himself but didn't woke up, his curiosity kicked in and he went inside the tall entrance of the market of midlife, it was very noisy, he saw people arguing with the stall owners, there were stalls on both sides on the road, brightened by the all-encompassing bright light above. The first stall had the highest amount of people trying to break a deal, Abhay went there, after squeezing through the crowd managed to ask the stall helper.

"Why is there so much crowd here?"

"We offer one of the most eye catching deal here" the stall helper answered.

"What is that?"

"Let go of your creativity, with money that would last a lifetime"

Abhay's face was rendered shocked, as he was pushed back by the hoard of people wanting to get ahead. On the road again he looked around and began to stroll, along the way he saw some shops where people were severing their hands for lifetime freedom from labour, giving up their freedom for physical pleasures, wandering through the passage he came across stalls where there was no one around, he went near and asked the stall keeper.

"What is the trade here?"

"In return of your wisdom you will gain ultimate recognition in the outside world" the stall keeper answered.

"Why is this empty?"

"People who possess the thing to be exchanged does not seem to fancy the trade"

"Seems fair" Abhay walked away with an intense look.

As he was walking away a sound fell on his ears

"Hello there, you seem to be a man of substance, we don't get much people like this here" A stall keeper shouted

"And what kind of person am I?" Abhay asked.

"We offer excellence in profession, popularity around the world, a beautiful partner, and immense amount of wealth, in exchange of nothing but your integrity"

"You have quite a price for that"

“Business is not booming though, as you can see, hardly anyone left with integrity now, you seem someone who maybe can afford the novelties”

“Thank you but I will pass” Abhay walked away without a second thought.

After wandering for a bit, he sat on a bench far from the stalls, just as he sat the man in robe came from behind.

“Not satisfied with the offers here?”

"I only crave for one thing in my life and I couldn’t find a single shop offering that" Abhay said in a low voice.

“And what do you crave for?”

“Love, I want love in my life, I can’t find someone offering that here, can you guide me?”

“Here you won’t find love, that is something we don’t sell or rather can’t sell, we don’t have anything that can be the price of something so pure, you must give love in order to receive the same, not a thrilling business possibility I assume”

Hearing this Abhay rose with hope in his eyes and told the man in robe.

“I want nothing from here, or at least nothing what you are selling, thank you so much, take me back”

As Abhay spoke these words he woke up suddenly in his bed with a smile on his face and a new perspective towards his life, he organized a party at his house and called all his colleagues to celebrate his birthday, he began to talk more to people, he knew that the most important thing is what he already has he just had to realize it.

CHAPTER SEVEN

The Mistake I Love

"The banner over this podium says, 'love and life' but there should be an 'or' in between (the crowd laughs), laughter... is interesting, you can't control it, maybe it's physical form sometimes, but not that feeling, urge to laugh, how many of you think the effect is same with love (most of the people in crowd raised their hands) all of you who have their hands pointing to sky are correct and to all those who think otherwise that they have control over love have either not been touched by love or it is love that has seasoned them, in any case we must know how important it is to us, but as every other thing we have developed ways to over complicate a simple concept, we all know number line right, it has negatives, 0 and positives, when we are born we have a neutral perspective of everything, 0, and as we grow up we develop positive and negative perspectives of the environment around us, we gain experience by that, but what we lose is the ability to go back to zero again, and that is too much of a prize believe it or not, every new consequence in our lives will have a prejudice associated, sometimes it helps, sometimes it doesn't , but this concept does not work with love, if you have been hurt in the past by someone it doesn't mean the next one is going to do the same, it is very important to have a new start, easier said than done I know, but it will save you great misery, with that said I must add that the only ones who can hurt you are the ones that you let, I hope that is clear especially to all those who kept their hands down(laughs), thank you for being such a nice audience and giving me as chance to speak midst these other great speakers"

The whole crowd rose and applauded what fell on their ears, but Melissa's eyes were glued on an attractive man who was looking at the podium in disgrace without applauding. The event concluded, everybody made their way toward the exit, except the charming personality who sat on a bench in the corner of the auditorium with a hand to his head, Melisa couldn't resist as she went there and sat beside him, the man sensed it and said in a deep voice without looking up.

"I told you it's all a lie and won't do any good."

"You sound like you've been hurt." Melissa said.

The man looked up sensing a different voice and apologized

"Sorry.., I thought there was someone else." and looked away again.

"I am also waiting for someone...." Melissa spoke in a shallow tone but the man didn't replied.

A few moments passed and Melissa said with hopeful eyes.

"I am Melissa Miller, you?"

"Nathan Brown, nice to meet you." he spoke without looking.

"So in the event which states 'Love and Life', what brings you here, like I just had a bad breakup and seeking guidance."

Nathan looked at his watch and then looked up to the empty auditorium, then said

"I would rather not talk about that."

“Come on, it looks like for whoever you are waiting is not going to be here for some time, we can talk and see how time flies by.”

“Okay, I am here because my sister for whom I am waiting forced me to be here against my will, as she believes that I will die alone.”

“Ohhh.... and why would she think so?”

“You can ask her that when she arrives.”

After some time a woman arrived at the bench.

“Ah, finally Eva, what took you so long.” Nathan spoke.

“Just was a bit busy with the organizers sorry, Nathan.”

“Happens” Eva’s eyes fell on Melissa and said.

“Melissa, what a pleasant surprise, it is to see you.”

“Oh Eva is that you, It has been so long.”

“You two know each other?” Nathan asked.

“Yes, we were together in collage and since then have been out of touch as she changed states.” Eva answered.

“And that I regret, how about we get together again like old times?” Melissa asked Eva.

“Sure why not, here take my number and we’ll catch up.”

“Agreed.” Melissa said while noting down the number.

After a few days they both decided to meet at Eva's apartment, the evening was cloudy with light showers passing by, Melissa knocked on the door drenched in her coat.

"You are on time." Eva said opening the door.

"The rain did try to hinder me." Melissa smiled.

"Come on in, get changed there are my clothes in the closet."

"Sure" Melissa said by making her way toward the washroom looking around the apartment trying to find someone.

Finishing the shower Melissa entered the hall and asked Eva.

"Nathan doesn't seem to be around I guess."

"Yes, he likes to live alone, he has a condo in downtown, that's where he lives."

"Oh!, I see."

"He did look a bit shattered at the auditorium."

"That's because had a breakup 4 months back, haven't recovered from it."

"Seems to be a long time to recover...."

"Yeah, he doesn't trust anyone easily and then when you finally put trust on someone and it is broken, it is very difficult to recover."

"I have got different view on this, I recover easily."

"Everyone is not created the same."

"I guess that's true."

"That is the reason I pushed him to attend the session, seems it didn't helped much."

"Don't be so sure."

"I sense something."

"To be honest, Eva, I have developed a liking for your broth...."

"I won't be able to help you in that, maybe he himself would fail in doing so" Eva interrupted Melissa.

"The only help I am asking from you is can you peruse him just for a coffee date between me and him, please, is that not what you want?"

"The only point of question is, what he wants, I will try but don't guarantee anything."

"Works for me" Melissa nodded as her face couldn't suppress the happiness.

On that same weekend Nathan and Melissa decide to meet at a local cafe, the day was shining bright, the street was less busy than usual, Nathan came and sat at the table.

"You are early." Nathan said.

"I didn't wanted to miss out." Eva smiled.

Nathan returned the smile in a sarcastic way.

"Eva told it would be tough to set this up." Melissa said.

“She would be able to better answer that question, see Melissa I don’t find a glitch in you but that is no reason to be together, so I appreciate you taking this time, but sorry this can’t be.”

“Don’t reach at conclusions so early Nathan.”

“This is more if a decision.”

“I hear you are an investment banker, make an investment in me, I wouldn’t expect anything in return more than love.”

“I don’t make investments in love, not for returns. If you may excuse me now” Nathan said by getting up from the chair.

“Wait Nathan, I know what you’ve been through....”

"YOU!, have no idea, what she did" Nathan shouted, Melissa’s eyes were glued to him in shock.

“She broke my trust, she broke me.” Nathan said while sitting down.

“I would never do that.”

“Why should I trust you.”

“Because that is the only way, give me a chance, give yourself a chance, that is all I am asking for.”

Nathan looked away.

“Trust me, I won’t break it, and I am not asking for any commitments from your end, If anyone wants out they can, if this doesn’t work out”

"Sounds good" Nathan agreed.

The next day Melissa moved to Nathan's condo, Melissa was a pediatrician, they both mostly spent their days at work and arrived late at night from their work, but every night they talked for hours about their life choices, personalities, each other, love and time went by.

It had been more than 4 months now, both of them found pace and place in the relationship, both were compatible with each other strengths and weaknesses, it seemed both knew that they were made for the other half. A night arrived with thunderous storm, when visibility and darkness were alike with just the thunders making an exception, Nathan and Melissa were at the condo, as Melissa made coffee for Nathan and brought it to him, Nathan said

"I want to ask you something today."

"Yes go ahead." Melissa nodded.

"These four months has been the most beautiful time of my life, you have made me better, I feel it time has come to confess, I love you, Melissa" Nathan said by showing her an engagement ring, Melissa was shocked with her eyes sparking shades of emotions.

"But there is no enforcement here, you can opt out of this if you like, no pressure, just as you said."

"I love you too Nathan, only a fool to turn down a man like you" Melissa said with eagerness and hope.

"Then it is decided, we will be arrange a wedding shortly"

"Yes we will".

Both of them hugged each other as the night eloped the moon in all its elegance.

The day had come for wedding, Melissa was ready in her white gown, sitting at her dressing table, she called for Nathan.

“Here you are, looking beautiful as ever in that white dress, today the day has came where we would be together forev....”

“Nathan, I wanted you to know something” Melissa said in a nervous voice.

“What is it love?” Nathan asked.

“Nathan when you asked to be together forever, I didn’t wanted to lose you, you are perfect, but I don’t know, this weeding is too much for me to take right now.”

“What are you talking about? don’t do this to me, please”

“I don’t want to, believe me, but the time is not right for us”.

“How can you do this!”

“Please try to under....”

“Say no more, you’ve lost me today.” Nathan walked out.

Fifteen years had passed until then, Melissa was on a tour for his company, midst the expo she heard a voice from an auditorium nearby, the word “Love” grabbed her attention, she listened closely.

“I used to believe, no one was created for me and I was right no one is, but not just for me, for each of us it is true, there is no soul mate, there are just people who are good enough for you with whom you can bear the hardships and share the joys of your life, and there is more than one person in the world who suffices that, but one is all you'll ever need, destiny is kind to some of the people, for others not so much, I myself have been slaughtered from the hands of people I so dearly loved....love, but that has made me stronger, It is true you don't have control over love, but if what you love is pure you don't need control, Thank you all"

She found the voice familiar, and rushed to the auditorium, on the podium she saw no one speaking, looking around she found no one, as a voice approached from the back.

"Looking for someone?"

"Nathan!!" she exclaimed looking around.

"I was told that I have a rational audience, seems that was a lie" Nathan smiled.

"You here?.... how? I never imagined you would take up this profession" Melissa asked, trying to adjust to the reality.

"Imagination is fragile, actions are not. You left me in sorrow, pain, disgust and I learnt their value, which I now share with the people"

"I tried to find you after that, you were not to be found anywhere"

"I didn't wanted to be found again, at least not that version of me"

"I haven't loved anyone since then, have you taken up a partner?" Melissa said in a sobbing voice.

"Nope"

"So are you planning to have a family?"

“As I said, you just have to find the right person”

“You know I regret my decision...., just give me another chance, can we be back toget....”

“You know I still love you and I love you so much that I can let you walk away with a smile and don’t need to regret anything, cause I can’t; not now, I learn from my mistakes and move forward and that is what you are to me ‘The mistake I love’”.

9 798887 492940

Printed by Libri Plureos GmbH in Hamburg,
Germany